Why _{is} Nita

Upside Down?

Written by Roxana Bouwer
Illustrated by Sarah Bouwer
Designed by Emma Hearne

Library For All is an Australian not for profit organisation with a mission
make knowledge accessible to all via an innovative digital library solutio
Visit us at libraryforall.org

Why is Nita Upside Down?

Published by Library For All 2021

Published by Library For All Ltd
Email: info@libraryforall.org
URL: libraryforall.org

This publication is a translation of the original, Why is Nita Upside Down?
Illustrated by Sarah Bouwer
Written by Roxana Bouwer
Designed by Emma Hearne
Originally published by Book Dash (bookdash.org) in 2017 under a
Creatives Common CC BY 4.0 license.
This edition was made possible by the generous support of the Educatio
Cooperation Program.

Why is Nita Upside Down?
Bouwer, Roxana
ISBN: 978-1-922550-02-6
SKU01559

Why is Nita Upside Down?

Nita's hanging upside down,
her long hair tickling at the ground.

The trees, the grass, the everything
is all the wrong way round.

3

Her feet, they poke into the sky.
Little Navi's walking by.

He says 'I've seen you here before.
You're upside down again! What for?'

His feet swim lightly in the air.
She tries to hide behind her hair.

'It's h-h-h-hard to t-t-talk', she says to him.
'I'm not the same. I don't fit in.'

Navi takes her by the hand.
He wants to help her understand.

They climb to Navi's look-out spot.
From up here they can see a lot.

They perch and have a quiet stare
at children playing here and there.

Those kids are not
the same at all.

Abe's round.

Chi's freckled,

Lala's extra tall.

Bambam's wild and must be free,

while Lulu's reading quietly.

Look at Freya's crazy hair.

And Sid wears glasses everywhere.

And me, I am just skin and bone.
And you are you. You're not alone.

Each human's sort of strange, you see.
That makes you just the same, like me.

This world is really one big game.
To play, we can't all be the same.

Nita feels the right way round,
thanks to the new friend she's found.

Upside down was never fun.
Now she plays with everyone.

You can use these questions to talk about this book with your family, friends and teachers.

What did you learn from this book?

Describe this book in one word. Funny? Scary? Colourful? Interesting?

How did this book make you feel when you finished reading it?

What was your favourite part of this book?

About the contributors

Library For All works with authors and illustrators from around the world to develop diverse, relevant, high quality stories for young readers. Visit libraryforall.org for the latest news on writers' workshop events, submission guidelines and other creative opportunities

Did you enjoy this book?

We have hundreds more expertly curated original stories to choose from.

We work in partnership with authors, educators, cultural advisors, governments and NGOs to bring the joy of reading to children everywhere.

Did you know?

We create global impact in these fields by embracing the United Nations Sustainable Development Goals.

libraryforall.org

CPSIA information can be obtained
at www.ICGtesting.com
Printed in the USA
BVHW091357230421
605645BV00012B/466